# Chapter One

Murdo sat on the sofa with his feet up, staring at the telly. It was darts. "One hundred and *eighty*!" said the commentator.

"Nice throwing," said Murdo's dad, who was keen on darts. Murdo's mum was doing the ironing, and didn't say anything, just looked across at them in a disapproving sort of way. Any minute now, Murdo thought, she'd start nagging at him to do something more active. She had a thing about him being too fat and not doing enough exercise.

It all started when she'd overheard Murdo's friend, Ian, calling him Fatso. It was only a joke – but Murdo's mum had taken it seriously.

Murdo had started it all when he'd called Ian Mouse Muck, because Ian had these white mice and when he cleaned their cage out, the smell made your eyes run. But Mouse Muck hadn't stuck and Fatso somehow had.

Murdo's mum was quite upset about it.

She'd made Murdo come to her yoga class, hoping it would help him get thinner. He'd quite enjoyed it, especially the bit where you lay down on a mat and relaxed. He'd gone on relaxing for the rest of the evening, while everyone else got themselves twisted into

knots and tried to look calm about it, and his mum hadn't taken him again.

He looked down at himself and sighed. He *was* quite big. But then, so was his dad, and nobody called him Fatso. He was just large and strong. He did removals, loading people's furniture into his van and unloading it in their new house.

Murdo's mum wouldn't have dreamed of hauling *him* along to her tap-dancing class – but she'd made Murdo come, and it was terrible.

The class was taken by Miss Joy, who wore red shoes and a bow in her hair. She gave Murdo a big smile and said, "Tap is wonderful for losing weight – just look at Jeremy." Jeremy was the only other boy in the class. He was so skinny,

8

he might have been made from
a model aircraft kit, Murdo
thought, with balsa wood for
arms and legs. He scowled
at Jeremy,

and Jeremy
scowled back.

Then Miss Joy had switched on the tape recorder and everyone started to dance. They hopped up and down and shuffled and tapped, and Murdo got hopelessly out of breath, and didn't know what to do with his feet. The shuffle and tap were all right, but he couldn't do those and hop at the same time.

So he'd found a little gilt chair
and sat down on it to practise
the feet bit without the
hopping, and got on better
that way. Then the chair broke,
and Miss Joy had been cross.

So had Murdo's mum.
Going home on the bus, she'd
scolded him. "You just don't
try, Murdo, that's your trouble.
You're lazy. You'll never get
slimmer if you don't try."

Murdo didn't want to try.
There was no point. He'd be all
right once he was grown up,
he thought, like his dad. He'd
know things like how to drive
and how to play darts, and
nobody would
call him
Fatso.

But that was a long way off.
Right now, he was sitting on
the sofa in front of the telly.
The darts had stopped and
now sumo wrestling was on.

Two huge
Japanese
men were
prowling
round each
other with their
knees a bit bent
and their hands out,
making grunting noises. This
went on for some time, until
one of them made
a dart at the
other and they
both fell on
the floor and
everyone
cheered and
clapped.

Funny, thought Murdo. Why didn't someone try to make *them* lose weight? The pair of them were enormous.

Murdo mentioned this to his dad, who said, "They've got to be big. Put someone skinny in the ring with those two, he'd be squashed as flat as the ham in a sandwich. Speaking of which," he added, "how about a little snack?"

"It's only an hour since tea," said Murdo's mum.

But his dad went and raided the fridge, and came back with a plate of cold sausages and several slices of bread and a big lump of cheese.

"Got to keep your strength up," he said.

## *Chapter Two*

The next day, Murdo's mum
met him from school and took
him swimming. Murdo quite
liked that – it was very restful.
He floated on his back, looking
up at the ceiling while everyone else dived and splashed,
and tanked up and down
doing lengths.

The day
after,
Murdo's
mum took
him to
aerobics instead,
where people
in leotards
got on
and off little steps about the size
of a brick – but even she

admitted that it
was boring.
She tried to get
him interested
in jogging,
but he didn't jog,
just walked,

18

and in the end they had to get the bus home. Sitting beside him, Murdo's mum said, "Maybe you're not cut out for dynamic exercise."

Murdo stared out at a passing fish-and-chip shop and made no reply. If dynamic meant hurling yourself about, she was dead right.

"You don't mind walking, though, do you?" his mum went on.

"It's better than jogging," Murdo said cautiously. "Or tap."

His mum nodded several times. "That's what I thought," she said.

For the next couple of days there were no more attempts to get him to exercise, and Murdo hoped she'd given up.

But at breakfast on Saturday morning, his mum said, "I've been talking to Aurora – you know, the woman with all those dogs."

"Off her head," said Murdo's
dad. "She's always
taking them
for walks.
In the rain,
even."

Murdo's mum nodded eagerly. "That's just what I mean," she said. "Long walks, every day. With a dog, there's no choice, you've absolutely got to go out. And Aurora's ever so slim. She says it's because of the dogs. She gets lots of exercise without even noticing."

"Same with darts," said Murdo's dad. "I reckon I walk miles, to and from that board. Not to mention the actual throwing. Terrific exercise for the arm."

"The darts players are really ginormous," Murdo said.

"Ah, well, you need
a bit of weight," said his dad.
"Gives you a good solid base.
Feet well planted on the
ground, you see."

Murdo's
mum sighed.
"Look," she
said, "I'm
trying
to think
of a way
to get
Murdo a
bit slimmer.
You're no
help, are
you?"

"Murdo's all right as he is," said his dad. And Murdo smiled at him. His mum kept on about dog walks, though.

"I'm sure that's the answer," she said. "Nice, gentle exercise every single day, even if it's raining or snowing. Dogs have to have walks. Aurora says it's essential."

So that afternoon, Murdo and his mum set out for the pet shop.

Murdo was not too happy about walking a dog. "Can't it just run round the garden?" he asked.

"No, it can't," said his mum. "I mean, just look at our garden – it's only big enough for the dustbin and the whirly thing to hang the washing on.

And a dog – well, I mean, it needs to – um – do things. Aurora says you have to have a pooper scooper, in case it does things on the pavement."

"Ugh!" said Murdo "Yukky." His dad was right, he thought. Aurora was definitely off her head.

## Chapter Three

The pet shop
had some
puppies that
were fast
asleep in a
nest of straw

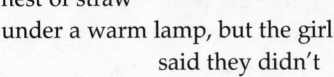

under a warm lamp, but the girl
said they didn't
have any
z-z-z-grown-up
dogs. "You
could try the
Rescue Home,"
she said. "They've always got
lots there."

But
Murdo was
looking at
something
else. From
between the
bars of a cage,
a pink nose and
quivering white whiskers
looked out. He tickled the nose,
and a neat
little white
paw with
pink claws
gripped his
finger.

"Hallo,"
he said. "Aren't you nice!"

28

"What have you got there?" asked his mum.

"It's a rat," said Murdo. Look, he's got a long pink tail."

"She," corrected the pet shop girl. "It's a girl rat. We had lots, but she's the only one left. We call her Rosie because of her pink nose."

Murdo thought of Ian and the mouse muck. "Do rats smell?" he asked. "Not a bit," said the girl. They're very clean.

You have to keep their sawdust changed, of course – and don't give them too much cheese. Do you want to look at her? Come on, Rosie." She opened the cage and picked the rat up. "You can stroke her," she said. "She likes that."

"Can I hold her?" asked Murdo.

" 'Course you can. Be careful, though – don't drop her."

Murdo was very careful. Rosie felt nice – all quivery, and her white coat was very soft. She was quite fat, too. Her little pink claws gripped his hand, and after a minute she ran up his sleeve and sat on his shoulder, washing her face.

"Mum, could I have her instead of a dog?" asked Murdo. "Please!"

"You can't take a rat for walks," said his mum.

"You can, actually," said the pet shop girl. "Rats are very intelligent, you see – they love looking at new things."

Rosie put
her nose in
Murdo's
ear and
he felt her
whiskers tickling.

"I'll buy her with my pocket
money," he offered. "I've only
got seventeen
pence, but you
can stop giving
me any until
she's paid for."

"It's not the money," said his
mum. "It's just that – well, it
looks so silly, going home with
a rat instead of a dog. What's
your dad going to say?"

"He won't care," said
Murdo. "He's only interested
in darts."

"Oh, I don't know," said his
mum. "He likes his food as
well. But what about getting
you exercise?"

"I'll take Rosie for a walk
every day," Murdo promised.

"Even if it's raining. OK?"

His mum sighed. "OK," she said. So they went home with Rosie, complete with her cage and drinking-water bottle and a packet of rat food.

# Chapter 4

The next day was a Sunday, and Murdo took Rosie for a walk down to the park and back, but it rained and she didn't seem to like it much. She hid in his pocket with her paws over her nose. He knew exactly how she felt.

On Monday, he took her
to school. Ian was very
impressed.

"Heck of a size, isn't she," he
said. "Much bigger than a
mouse. Good old Fatso!" And
he gave Rosie a bit of his
apple, which she
ate up very neatly.

Their teacher, Mrs Bartlett, didn't seem too keen on Rosie. She gave a sort of shriek and stood with her hands up as if she'd seen something nasty.

Then she said school was definitely not the place for rats and Murdo was to leave her at home in future.

For the next few days, Murdo went on taking Rosie for a walk when he came home from school but neither of them enjoyed it much, so he played with her in his bedroom, which was much better. And his mother sighed.

The next Saturday morning,
Murdo's dad said, "Got a job
on today – house clearance.
D'you want to
come? You
could make
yourself
useful, carry
a few
things."

"Yes, please,"
said Murdo.
"Can I bring
Rosie?"
"Don't see
why not," his
dad said. "Long
as she doesn't get in the way."

Murdo promised she wouldn't, and they set off in the van. They stopped off to pick up Murdo's dad's mate, a rather silent man called Donald, then went on to the house. It was quite small, sandwiched between two others in a narrow street.

Murdo's dad and Donald went in through the front door.

They came
out again
with tables
and chairs

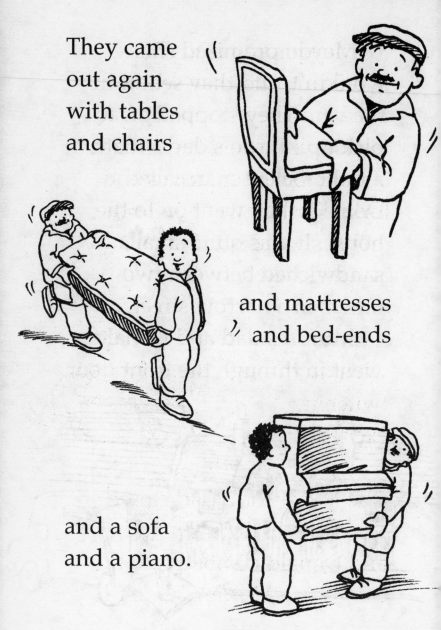

and mattresses
and bed-ends

and a sofa
and a piano.

They packed everything tightly into the van, while Murdo carried small things like fire-irons and the kitchen bin and boxes of knives and forks. Rosie rode on his shoulder and watched everything with her whiskers twitching excitedly.

At last everything was in. Murdo's dad closed the doors of the van and he and Donald climbed into the cab beside Murdo.

"Where does the stuff have
to go?" asked Murdo. "Have
the people moved to another
house?"

"No, it belonged to an old
lady," said his dad, "and she
passed away."

"What does 'passed away'
mean?" asked Murdo.

"Dead," said Donald.

"Oh."

"So I'll take it all home and shove it in the garage," said his dad. "Then I'll sort it out and sell the best of it. The rest can go in an auction sale later."

"I see," said Murdo. Then he gave a gasp as he realised something awful. Rosie wasn't on his shoulder. She wasn't in his pocket, either. He hunted frantically about, looking over the back of the seat and down the gap where the handbrake was.

"Lost something?" asked Donald.

"My rat. She's gone!"

"Probably in the back," said Murdo's dad. "She may have hopped in there when you put something in. Let's have a look."

He got out and opened the back doors of the van. It was absolutely stuffed with furniture. Murdo stared in.

"Rosie!" he called. There was no reply – but up near the van's roof, he saw the tip of a pink tail disappearing over the edge of a fringed lampshade.

"There she is!" he said.

"That's all right, then," said his dad. And he shut the van's doors again.

"But – "

"If you think I'm going to unload that lot just to get your rat out, you can think again.

She can't come to any harm in there. We'll find her when we get home." said his dad.

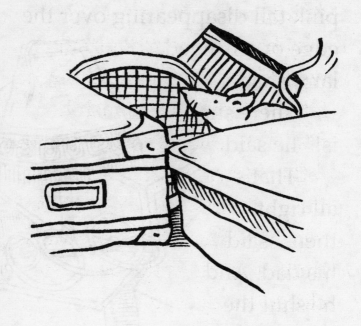

## Chapter Five

Murdo was not happy. All the way back to their house, he worried that something might fall on Rosie and squash her flat. Once, his dad had to brake rather sharply when a woman pushed a pram in front of the van, and Murdo heard things thump about in the back. He closed his eyes in terror.

When they got home, Murdo's dad said, "We'll unload after lunch. Fancy a game of darts, Donald?"

"Wouldn't mind," said Donald. So he and Murdo's dad headed off towards the Bull and Stag.

Murdo opened the rear doors of the van.

"Rosie?" he said. "Where are you?" He listened, but there was no sound. Very carefully,

he took
out a
rubber plant
in a brass pot,

then a stool
with feet,

then a couple
of cushions.

"Rosie?" he called again – but
there was no reply.

It was starting to drizzle a bit. Murdo thought the things he'd taken out of the van ought not to get wet, so he slid the garage doors open and put them inside. Then he took a standard lamp out of the van, and a wicker chair and a bathroom cupboard, and put

them in the garage as well. There was still no sign of Rosie.

He moved a box
of old records
and a record-
player and two
kitchen chairs,
then hauled
out a pile of
curtains. He
was getting
quite warm in
spite of the rain.

He carried all the things into
the back of the
garage, because
if he left them
just inside the
door, he'd trip
over them.

When he'd taken out a bookcase and a leather pouffe and a plywood kitchen cupboard, there was a lot more room and he could climb into the back of the van.

"Rosie!" he shouted. "Where have you gone?" Murdo thought he heard a very faint rustle.

Perhaps things had fallen about
on the journey, and she was
trapped in there somewhere.
She might not be able to get
out. He heaved a dining table
to the edge of the van and
lowered it carefully to the
ground, then pulled out a
writing desk. Both of those
were heavy, and by
the time he'd
got them into
the garage, his
face was red
and he was
quite hot and
sticky, but he
kept at it.

He unloaded
a roll of carpet,
lots of folded
blankets and
sheets and
pillows, two
bedside tables and four boxes
of books, then he
climbed into
the van and
listened again.
This time he
definitely heard
something – it was a shuffling
noise, a bit like someone
stirring up a lot of bits of
paper. It was coming from a
wastepaper basket, high up in

the corner, on top of a washing
machine. Murdo climbed up
the back of an armchair and
over the piano, and peered in.

"Rosie!" he said.

"*There* you are!"

# Chapter Six

The wastepaper basket was full
of saucepans and wrapped-up
cups and plates, and Rosie was
curled comfortably in a
cooking-pot full of torn-up
paper. She'd unwrapped quite

a lot of cups
to make
herself a
newspaper
nest, but nothing was broken.
She looked up at Murdo and
twiddled her whiskers, then
cuddled down again. Murdo
lifted her out in her cooking-
pot, and was just climbing
down from the van when his
dad and Donald appeared. "I
found her!" he said.

Neither of them answered.
They were both staring at the
almost empty van.

"Did you unload that lot?"
asked his dad. "On your own?"

"I was looking for Rosie," said Murdo.

"I know, but – heck," said his dad. "You must be strong."

"Sumo," said Donald. And they went in for lunch.

"Have you had a good morning?" Murdo's mum asked. Then she saw Murdo's hot, sweaty face and said, "Good heavens! What on earth have you been doing?"

"Unloaded the whole van on his own, just about," said his dad. "Stacked it all in the garage too. Never seen anything like it.

There'll be a job waiting for you, Murdo, soon as you've left school."

"Well, I never," said his mum. "Fancy you doing all that. No wonder you didn't like running and jumping – I expect you're a natural weight- lifter."

"Could be," said Murdo. "What's for lunch? I'm starving."

After that, Murdo helped his
dad most weekends, and his
mum stopped worrying about
him getting enough exercise.
Rosie produced a whole family

of little ratlets the day after her
trip in the van, and brought
them up in the cooking-pot.
By the time they had all found
good homes, she was quite
slim. Murdo was a bit slimmer
too, though not very much.

Ian came round one
Saturday, to help Murdo with
some unloading. And by the
time they'd finished, Murdo
wasn't being called Fatso
any more. From that day on,
Ian called him Sumo instead.